The Sparkle Egg

Written by Jill Hardie ∽ Illustrated by Christine Kornacki

ideals children's books.
Nashville, Tennessee

ISBN-13: 978-0-8249-5664-6

Published by Ideals Children's Books
An imprint of Ideals Publications
A Guideposts Company
Nashville, Tennessee
www.idealsbooks.com

Designed by Georgina Chidlow-Rucker

Color separations by Precision Color Graphics, Franklin, Wisconsin
Printed and bound in China

Leo_Nov14_2

This book is dedicated to my Lord and Savior, Jesus Christ. Thank You for teaching me that through You, all things are possible. —J.H.

*To James and all my PV friends,
for so many memorable years.—C.K.*

Library of Congress Cataloging-in-Publication Data

Hardie, Jill, date.
The Sparkle Egg / by Jill Hardie ; art by Christine Kornacki.
pages cm
Summary: Sam feels guilty after lying to his parents about a spelling test, but they teach him how an empty Easter egg, decorated with jewels, can symbolize accepting Jesus's forgiveness.
ISBN-13: 978-0-8249-5664-6 (hardcover : alk. paper) [1. Honesty—Fiction. 2. Forgiveness—Fiction. 3. Easter—Fiction. 4. Conduct of life—Fiction. 5. Christian life—Fiction.] I. Kornacki, Christine, illustrator. II. Title.
PZ7.H2176.Sr 2014
[E]—dc23

2013037259

Dear reader, may you accept the gift of God's grace—and shine!

✣ ✣ ✣ ✣ ✣

Sam stared at the line of red *X*'s on his spelling test in disbelief. He had never done so poorly on a test before. The teacher handed a paper with a gold star on it to his best friend and told him to hang it on the wall for the Spring Open House.

Sam slid his paper under his books before anyone could see it. For the rest of the school day, Sam worried what his parents would say when they heard about his test.

When he got home from school, Sam discovered cups of blue, green, yellow, purple, and orange dye sitting on the table. His spirits lifted. Coloring eggs was one of his favorite Easter traditions!

Carefully balancing an egg on the holder, Sam began to lower it into a cup of brilliant blue dye. This was going to be his masterpiece!

"So how did you do on your spelling test?" his mom asked.

The egg splashed into his cup. "I got a gold star on it, but I left it at school!" he blurted out.

"That's great, honey. I'm proud of you!"

Sam quickly got up from the table and grabbed Duke's leash.

Duke stopped to sniff the spring flowers that were beginning to poke through the ground. Sam urged him along, kicking a rock as they walked.

He thought about how he lied to his mom. He felt sick inside. Ashamed.

Sam knelt down. Duke licked his nose and nuzzled his face, but Sam didn't feel any better.

The next night, Sam and his parents went to the Spring Open House at his school. He was excited to show his parents around his classroom.

Sam's mom stopped to look at the spelling tests posted on the wall. "Sam, I can't find your test, the one you got a gold star on," she commented.

Sam felt a hand on his shoulder. He looked up—right into the eyes of his teacher!

"Sam didn't do well on his test," she told his mom. "But we can talk about that later. Right now, it's time for refreshments in the gym."

Sam's cheeks were burning as everyone but Sam and his parents left the room.

1 2 3
7 8 9
14 15
21 22
28 29

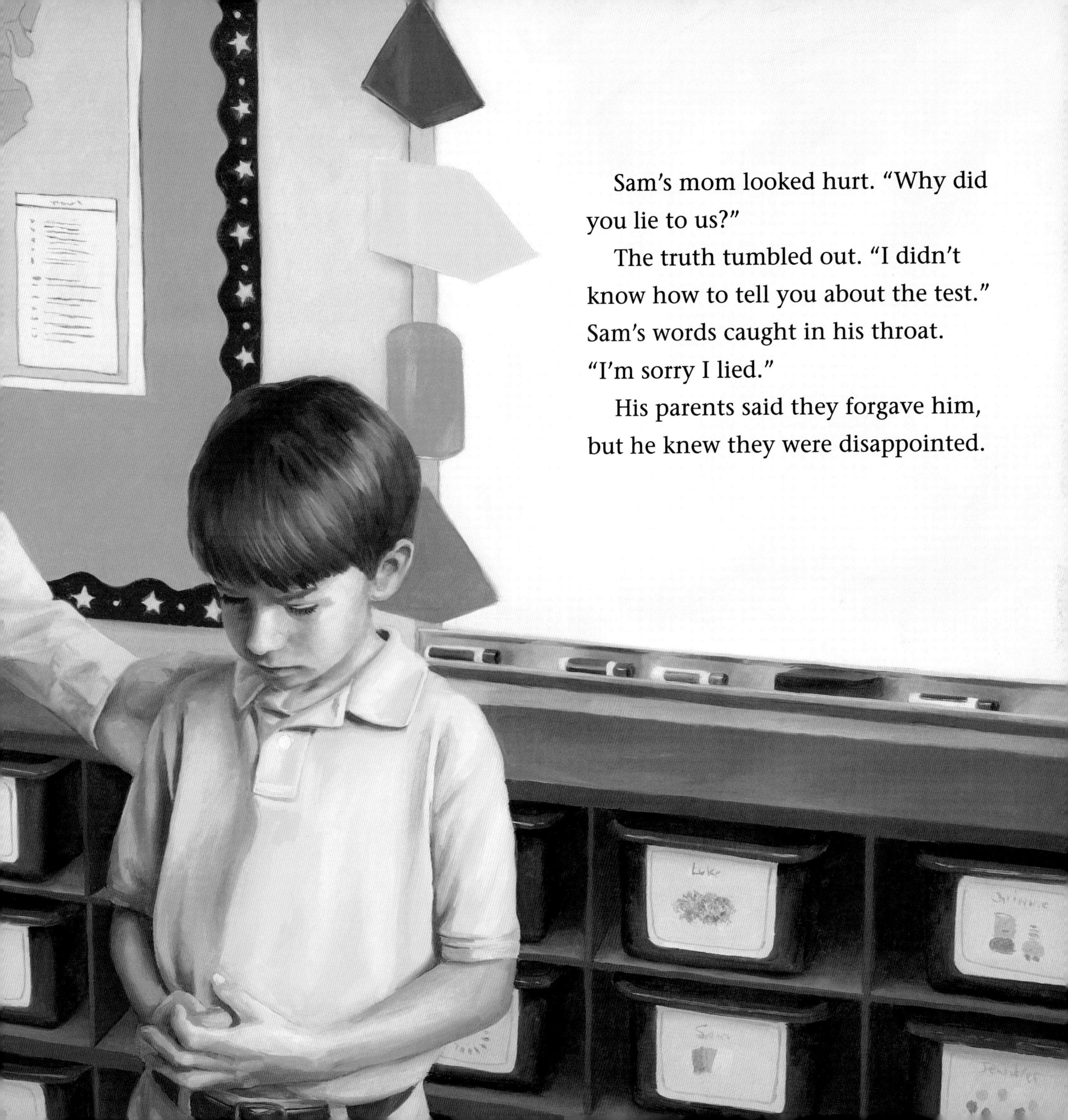

Sam's mom looked hurt. "Why did you lie to us?"

The truth tumbled out. "I didn't know how to tell you about the test." Sam's words caught in his throat. "I'm sorry I lied."

His parents said they forgave him, but he knew they were disappointed.

That week, Sam had trouble sleeping.

His dad poked his head into Sam's room. "Are you still awake?"

In the dark, Sam nodded.

His dad sat down on the edge of his bed. "Sam, you haven't seemed like yourself the past couple of days. Are you okay?"

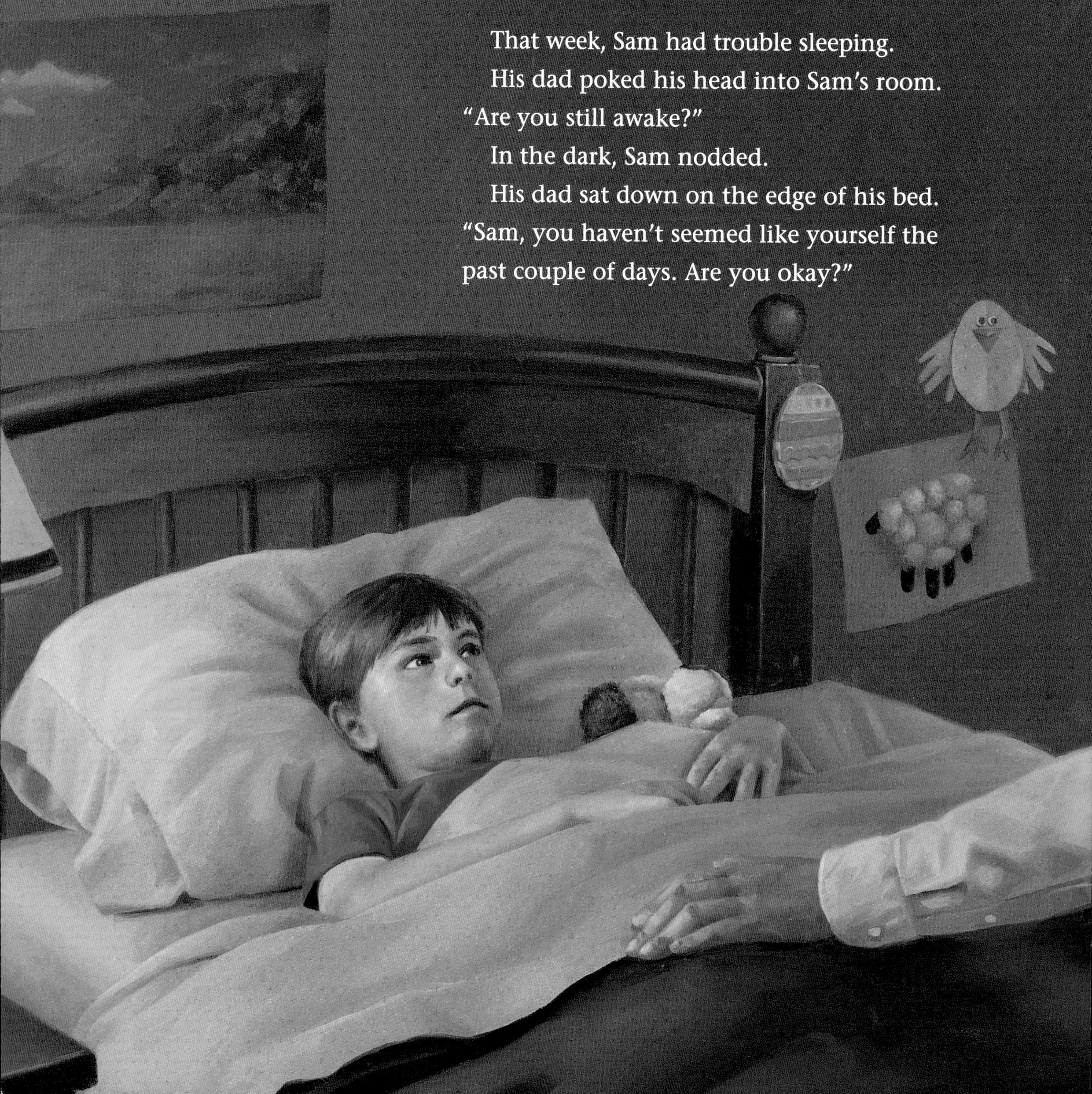

Sam was quiet for a moment. "I just don't feel like a good kid."

"Is this about the spelling test?" he asked.

Sam nodded.

"You know, everyone messes up sometimes," Sam's dad said gently. "The important thing is to ask the people that you've hurt for forgiveness and to pray and ask God for His forgiveness too."

Even though he had already done those things, Sam still felt bad. He rolled to his side and faced the wall. He didn't want his dad to see his tears.

The next day, it was Good Friday. Sam's mom announced they were going to make a special Easter craft, called a Sparkle Egg, to honor Jesus.

Sam was excited! He covered his egg with colorful, shiny jewels.

When he was finished, his mom gave him a slip of paper.

"I want you to draw a picture of anything you're ashamed of, or that you feel guilty about, on this slip of paper and put it in the egg. Only you need to know what the picture means."

Sam thought of how he lied about getting a star on his spelling test. He drew a star on his paper.

He folded the paper and put it inside the Sparkle Egg.

His dad sat beside Sam and his mom. He took Sam's hand and led them in prayer. "Dear God, we ask forgiveness for the things we've done wrong. We thank You that because of Your Son, Jesus, we are forgiven."

"Now what do we do?" Sam asked his parents.

"Now we wait until Easter morning," his mom replied. "When you wake up, there will be something special in your Sparkle Egg that will honor Jesus."

Sam woke up bright and early on Easter morning and raced to the kitchen. His Easter basket was filled with colorful treats, chocolates, and a new kite! He couldn't wait to fly it!

But first, he wanted to find out what was inside the Sparkle Egg. He picked it up and carefully opened it.

"My egg is empty!" cried Sam.

Sam's mom explained, "The Sparkle Egg reminds us that Jesus died on the cross for our sins. And because He rose again on Easter, we are forgiven. Your egg is empty because the things you've done wrong are forgiven and gone—like the tomb was empty that first Easter Day."

"But Mom, you said the Sparkle Egg honors Jesus on Easter. How does it honor Him?"

Sam's dad said, "Jesus loves us so much that He died on the cross for us. The greatest gift of Easter is the gift of forgiveness through Jesus Christ. God doesn't want you to carry around guilt or feel ashamed—He wants you to feel His forgiveness in your heart." He said gently, "The best way we can honor Jesus' gift of forgiveness is to fully accept it.

"When we ask for forgiveness, but we still hold onto feelings of guilt and shame, we can't fully shine for God. We're too busy thinking about what we did wrong and feeling bad about it."

As Sam listened to the Easter story at church that morning, he thought about how terrible he had felt the past few days. He knew his dad was right. When he held onto his guilt, he wasn't shining for Jesus.

He decided that from now on, when he prayed for forgiveness, he would honor Jesus' sacrifice by accepting it one hundred percent.

That afternoon, as Sam flew his new kite, he thought about how it felt to be completely forgiven. He laughed as the wind blew in his face.

Running through the grass with Duke at his feet, he felt the blessing of forgiveness. He was free.

A NOTE FROM THE AUTHOR

You can make your own Sparkle Egg!

When you do something wrong, you may feel like you are a bad person, or like God doesn't love you anymore. Nothing could be further from the truth! God loves you no matter what! Because Jesus rose again on Easter Day, you are forgiven.

Sam's parents removed the paper from his Sparkle Egg to remind him that he was completely forgiven. Sam was holding onto his guilt and it was weighing him down. But when he accepted God's gift of forgiveness, he felt free. When we are free from the burden of guilt, we are able to let God's beautiful light shine through us.

Make your own Sparkle Egg by decorating a plastic egg with gems, glitter, or stickers. If you are having trouble accepting God's forgiveness for something you've done, draw a symbol that represents what you feel bad about and put it in your Sparkle Egg. On Easter morning, remove it from the egg to symbolize the empty tomb, and as a reminder that you are forgiven. Place the Sparkle Egg where you will see it every day to remember the gift of forgiveness—the gift of Easter!

"For God so loved the world that he gave his only Son, so that everyone who believes in him will not perish but have eternal life."

—John 3:16 (NLT)

But if we confess our sins to him, he is faithful and just to forgive us and to cleanse us from every wrong.

—1 John 1:9 (NLT)